THIS CANDLEWICK BOOK BELONGS TO:

_____

_____

_____

_____

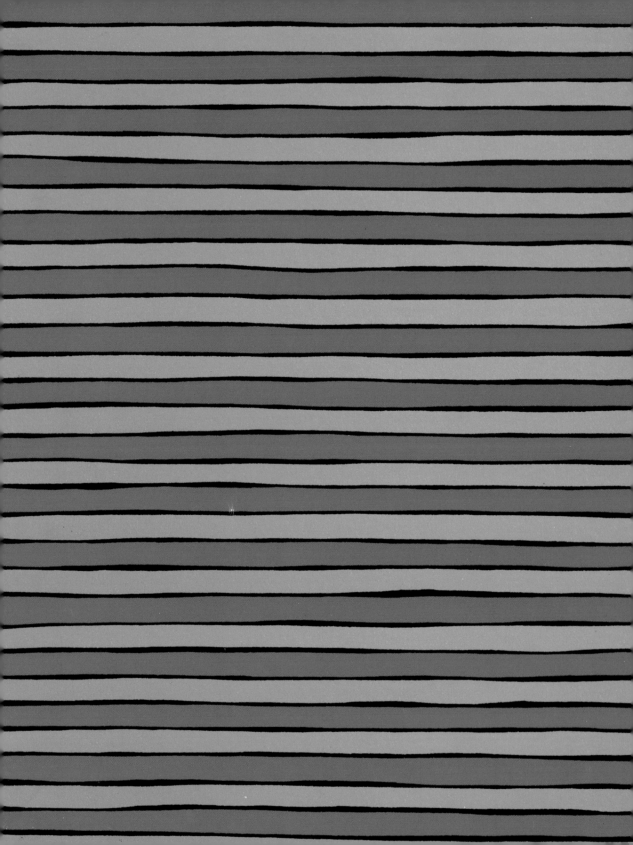

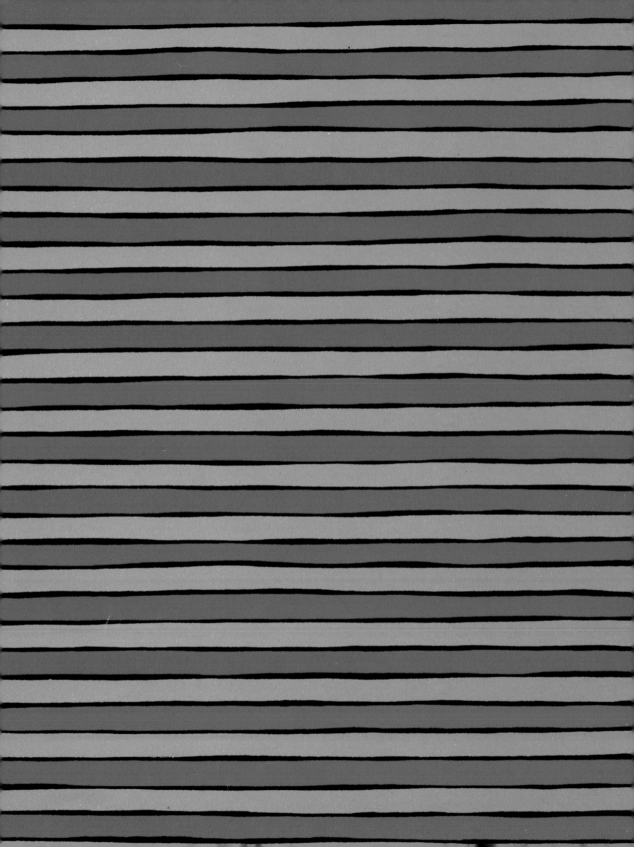

First U.S. edition 1996

Library of Congress Cataloging-in-Publication Data

Hindley, Judy.
Crazy ABC / Judy Hindley ; illustrated by Nick Sharratt.—
1st U.S. ed.
Summary: Presents objects and activities for each letter of the alphabet,
from an apple tree to a sleeper zipped up in a sleeping bag.
ISBN 1-56402-682-5 (alk. paper)
1. English language—Alphabet—Juvenile literature.
[1. Alphabet.]   I. Sharratt, Nick, ill.   II. Title.
PE1155.H52   1996
[E]—dc20   95-9498

2 4 6 8 10 9 7 5 3 1

Printed in Hong Kong

This book was typeset in Garamond Book Educational.
The pictures were done in watercolor and ink.

Candlewick Press
2067 Massachusetts Avenue
Cambridge, Massachusetts 02140

Crazy
ABC

Judy Hindley
illustrated by
Nick Sharratt

CANDLEWICK PRESS
CAMBRIDGE, MASSACHUSETTS

Aa

Ax in the apple tree—

what else begins like that?

Ask an alligator

with an apple

on his hat.

Bb

What can you see

that starts with *b?*

I see three things like that:

a thing that can sing,

a thing that can sting,

and a bat.

Boo, bee! You bother me!

Scat, bat!

Cc

Can you? Can you?

Can you do what I can do?

Can you creep along

like a caterpillar?

Can you curl up

like a cat?

Dd

What do you do

that starts with *d?*

What do you do, my dear?

I dance until I'm dizzy

with a daisy

in my ear.

Ee

Eh, eh, eh,

what have we here?

Egg on the edge,

egg on its end,

egg on my elbow—

egg everywhere!

Ff

Fie! Fo!

There's a fly on my nose!

What other funny things

can you see?

A frog on my foot,

a flea on my knee!

Gg

Gooey goose gravy—isn't it good?

Glassful of grape juice—glug, glug, glug.

Hh

Ho, ho, ho!

How shall I be happy?

I'll hop until I'm happy,

I'll hide until you find me,

and then I'll have a hug.

Ho, ho, ho!

Ii

"Ick!" said the Indian.

"It

is

ITCHY

in

this

outfit!"

Jj

What do you like

that starts with *j?*

Do you like Jell-O?

Do you like jam?

Do you like to jump

as high as you can?

Kk

Here is a kite

fit for a king!

Here is a king

in the kite string.

Give it a kick!

Ll

Look, look,

look what I can do!

Leap high . . .

Lie low . . .

Lick a large lollipop.

Mm

The mountaineer

has lost his map.

What a mess!

What a muddle!

Oh, where is his mom?

Nn

No, no, no!

This isn't nice!

Here is a ninny

with a nut on his nose

and a noodle on his necktie!

No, no, no!

Oo

Odd! It's an omelette—

an omelette falling off!

And here we see an officer

with omelette on top.

Pp

"Pooh!" said the pirate,

peering at his plate of prunes.

What a picky peg leg,

picking at his *p*s.

Can you find the *p*s?

Pickles, pears, potatoes—

look at all of these!

Qq

Queasy, queasy queen.

She must be feeling sick.

Tuck her in a quilt,

quick, quick, quick!

Rr

Rrrm, rrrm, racetrack rider,

racing for a ribbon,

roars around the racetrack,

rrrm, rrrm, rrrm!

Ss

See here! Sit up straight!

Sip your soup like Mrs. Snake.

Sssss—don't slurp!

What a silly sausage!

Tt

Tut, tut, tut,

do you have a *t?*

I have lots of *t*s:

tummy, toes, and teeth!

Uu

Up, up, up!

Underneath umbrella.

Upset,

upside down,

making ugly faces.

Vv

Vroom! Vroom!

Very fast van!

Very smashed vegetables,

very sad man.

Ww

Woo, woo, wild wind

whistles around your head.

Wiggly worm,

wicked witch,

warm in bed.

Xx

X ray.

Exit.

Who's next?

Yy

Yippee, yippee! Yellow yacht,

racing around the bend.

Happy, happy yachtsman

when the day is at an end.

Zz

Zipping in,

zipping up.

ZZZZZZZzzzzzz.

Good night, my friend.

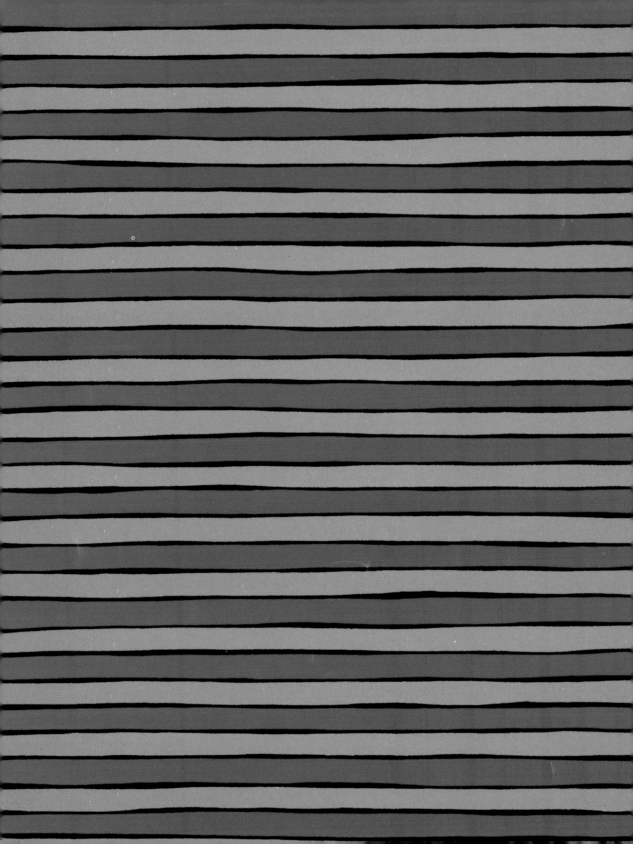

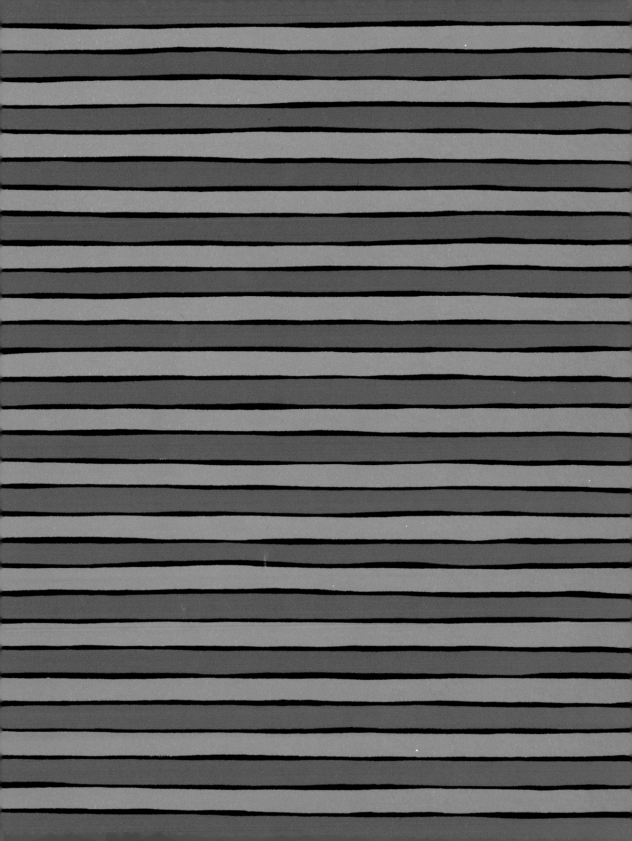

JUDY HINDLEY, a graduate of the University of Chicago, has written more than thirty books for children, including *A Piece of String Is a Wonderful Thing* and *The Wheeling and Whirling-Around Book*, both Candlewick Read and Wonder books, as well as *Into the Jungle*. She says this book is "meant to be read aloud; to be shared by a child and an adult. Children learn best when they're having fun *with* someone."

NICK SHARRATT loves striking patterns and bold colors, as is evident in his vibrant books *Rocket Countdown*, *My Mom and Dad Make Me Laugh*, *Monday Run-Day*, *The Green Queen*, *Snazzy Aunties*, and *Mrs. Pirate*. He comments that illustrating Judy Hindley's books was "really enjoyable; I felt completely in tune with Judy's poetry."